This edition published by Parragon Books Ltd in 2016

Parragon Books Ltd
Chartist House
15–17 Trim Street
Bath BA1 1HA, UK
www.parragon.com

Childhood Times written by Victoria Saxon, concept by Brittany Candau
Olaf's Perfect Summer Day written by Jessica Julius
Babysitting the Troll Tots and *Across the Sea* written by Brittany Candau
Melting Hearts written by Suzanne Francis
All stories illustrated by the Disney Storybook Art Team

ISBN 978-1-4748-3667-8

Printed in China

STORYBOOK
COLLECTION

Bath • New York • Cologne • Melbourne • Delhi
Hong Kong • Shenzhen • Singapore

Contents

CHILDHOOD TIMES

One day, when Elsa and Anna were little, the sun was shining in Arendelle. Two visiting ships were anchored in the harbour, and King Agnarr and Queen Iduna proudly greeted their guests. If all went well, then Arendelle would have two new partners in trade by the end of the visit.

Upstairs, Elsa and Anna stared in amazement at their breakfast.

"We get chocolate just because there are some fancy visitors?" Anna asked.

"I suppose we could refuse to eat it," Elsa teased.

"No!" Anna chomped on her chocolate croissant. "Elsa, can we play with the magic?"

"We're supposed to stay in our rooms and not disturb the guests," Elsa said.

"Elsa, pleeeeease?" Anna begged. "We can hide. They won't ever see us! And besides, the castle is so clean now, if you don't do the magic, then it's like the shiny floors will be wasted –"

"Okay!" Elsa interrupted. "Let's play, but we have to be very quiet."

Together, the sisters sneaked out into the castle's grand hallway. The king and queen were still outside in the gardens with the visitors, so Elsa raised her hands high into the air – *WHOOSH!* The hallway instantly froze with glistening ice.

"Whee!" shouted Anna as she slid across the floor.

15

When the king and queen came indoors with their visitors,
Anna and Elsa quickly sneaked away into the room where
the castle artwork was kept. Nobody saw them!

"That was a close call!" Elsa whispered to Anna. "We need to be careful or we'll get in trouble."

"Okay!" said Anna. "But can we use magic to make some ice statues? Please, Elsa?"

Elsa paused for just a second – and then made an ice statue. Then she made some more! The sisters squealed with delight.

"And now we would like to show you some of Arendelle's best artwork ..." the king said from the hallway. Anna and Elsa looked at each other and gasped! They raced out of the art room and fled into the kitchen.

The king and queen led the tour directly into the art gallery. Anna and Elsa had gone, but their ice sculptures were still in place.

"Ah! I say!" the Baron of Snoob exclaimed. "These statues are extraordinary!"

His wife, the baroness, was less impressed. "Harumph!" she huffed.

In the kitchen, Elsa cut loose! She made huge amounts of snow and ice, and the sisters began a big, fun snowball fight.

"Hit that pan!" Elsa shouted.

Anna hit it with a flying snowball. "Woo-hoooo!"

The two girls were having so much fun that they barely saw the king and queen approaching with their royal visitors! Quickly, Anna and Elsa slipped up the back staircase before anyone saw them.

When the king and queen entered the kitchen, they were surprised to see all of the ice. But the royal visitors thought the snowballs were wonderful.

"Oh, my. This is just what we need on a warm summer's day!" exclaimed the baron, spooning the snow into a cup. "You must try it, my dear!"

The baroness just stared at her icy snow cone. "Harumph!"

"Ah, yes!" the king chuckled. "Ice is Arendelle's number one form of trade."

"Indeed! We harvest lots of ice from lakes up in the nearby mountains," the queen added.

Anna and Elsa ran through the rest of the castle. There was no stopping them now!

In the ballroom, Elsa made lots of snowy hills.

Both girls slid up into the air ...

... and then down again.
They even made snow angels!

25

Suddenly, the girls heard the guests outside the ballroom doors.
"Uh-oh!" Elsa said, startled. "We had better stop!"
"They almost saw us!" Anna chirped. Neither of the girls wanted
to get into trouble, so they raced back to their bedrooms.

Meanwhile, down in the ballroom, the king and queen gasped when they saw the snowy hills and the —

"Oof!" The baroness slipped and landed in a pile of snow.

"Oh, dear!" said the queen, as she and the king rushed to help their guest.

"Snow angels!" the baroness cried out. "I love snow angels. What a surprise!"

"I say," the baron chuckled. "The kingdom of Arendelle truly stops at nothing to please its visitors!"

Soon everyone was enjoying the snow and ice. The king and queen were delighted to see their visitors having so much fun. All the guests wanted to do business with Arendelle, which clearly was a very happy and fun kingdom!

After the visitors had gone to their rooms
for the night, the king and queen went
to check on their daughters.

Both girls appeared to be
sleeping soundly ...

... but as soon as they were alone, the girls opened their eyes.

"Elsa, do you want to play?" Anna asked.

"Anna, we can't! We're already going to be in trouble," Elsa said.

Anna leaned back on to her pillow and sighed. "Still...."

Then both girls said together, "It was SO worth it!"

A FROZEN ADVENTURE

The kingdom of Arendelle was a happy place, located next to a deep fjord. At night, the Northern Lights often lit up the skies in beautiful patterns. But the king and queen lived with a secret worry.

34

Their eldest daughter, Elsa, had magical powers. She could freeze things and create snow, even in summer!

Their youngest daughter, Anna, adored her older sister. The two loved to play together in the snowy playgrounds that Elsa created.

One night, Elsa's magic accidentally hit Anna.

The king and queen rushed the girls to the realm of the trolls for magical help. The trolls advised that Anna would recover, but also that Elsa's powers would get stronger, so she should learn to control them.

Back in Arendelle, Elsa struggled to stay in control of her powers at all times. She decided to stay away from Anna to keep her little sister safe.

The trolls had changed Anna's memories, so she didn't remember Elsa had magic powers. She grew up thinking that Elsa wanted nothing to do with her.

By the time Elsa was crowned queen, the sisters had grown apart. They hardly knew each other.

Having grown up mostly by herself, Anna had felt lonely for a long time.
So she was thrilled to meet handsome Prince Hans on the day of Elsa's coronation.

Anna and Hans liked each other right away. At the coronation party they danced and talked all night.

Anna thought it was a great idea to get engaged quickly. But Elsa reacted angrily. "How can you marry someone you've just met?" she asked.

Anna argued back. "I can't live like this any more!"

Then Elsa got upset and an icy blast shot from her hand – in front of everyone!

Worried that her secret was exposed – and afraid she would hurt someone –

Elsa fled from the castle. Everything froze behind her as she ran away.

Once Elsa climbed into the mountains, she calmed down.
All alone, she could let her powers out, for the first time ever!
She created whirls of snow, ice and even an ice palace.
She was able to be herself and it felt wonderful!

Meanwhile, Anna realized that Elsa had been acting distant for all those years because she had been hiding her magic. Anna decided to go after Elsa – now that her secret was out, there was nothing to keep them apart!

Anna headed up the mountain, but her horse threw her into the snow. Luckily, she was able to find shelter in a nearby shop.

Inside, Anna met a young man covered in frost. He was cross because he was an ice harvester and the snowstorm was ruining his business.

He also knew where the storm was coming from. That meant he could take Anna to Elsa!

Anna hired the young man, who was called Kristoff, to take her up
the North Mountain to find Elsa. His reindeer, Sven, came along, too.

As they neared the top of the mountain, the trio saw a beautiful
wintery landscape. Elsa had covered everything with stunning, sparkling ice.

Elsa had also created a snowman ... who was alive!

The snowman's name was Olaf and he was excited to hear that Anna planned to bring back summer, because he loved to dream about warm weather.

Olaf offered to take them to Elsa.

As the group continued on, they found the fantastic ice palace that Elsa had created.
Anna was impressed by her sister's powers, but she wanted Elsa to come home.

Elsa thought the people of Arendelle wouldn't accept her – and she was still afraid of hurting them. The two girls argued and Elsa started to lose control. A blast of ice accidentally shot from her hand and hit Anna in the chest!

50

Then Elsa created another snowman, named Marshmallow,
who was much bigger than Olaf. The snowman made sure that
Anna, Kristoff, Sven and Olaf left the mountain quickly!

51

Once they were safe, Kristoff noticed that Anna's hair was turning white. Kristoff took her to the trolls to see if their magic could help.

The trolls explained that Elsa's blast had hit Anna in the heart – and that soon she would freeze completely! But, they added, "An act of true love will thaw a frozen heart."

Olaf and Kristoff decided to hurry Anna back to Arendelle so she could get a true love's kiss from Hans.

Meanwhile, back in Arendelle, Hans had helped everyone during the storm. Then Anna's horse had returned to Arendelle without her! Hans took a group out to find Anna ... but found Elsa first. Elsa was forced to defend herself against some of the men. Finally, she was taken back to Arendelle – as a prisoner! Everyone thought she was dangerous.

Kristoff brought Anna to Arendelle, but Hans refused to kiss her. He didn't really love her! He only wanted to rule Arendelle, but he had to make sure the sisters were out of the way first.

Olaf realized that it was Kristoff who really loved Anna – so his kiss could still save her. Anna made her way towards Kristoff, but then she saw that her sister was in danger....

Anna threw herself in front of Elsa, just in time to block a blow from Hans' sword.

At that moment, Anna transformed into solid ice. The sword shattered against her icy body.

Stunned, Elsa threw her arms round Anna and cried. She didn't want to lose her sister.

Suddenly, Anna began to melt. Anna's act of true love for her sister meant that the spell was broken!

Then, Elsa realized it was fear that had caused her to lose control of her powers. Love could bring back summer!

The sisters hugged and promised to love each other and tell the truth from then on. The people of Arendelle had seen everything and they welcomed Elsa home.

Kristoff decided to stay with Anna in Arendelle and so did Olaf – with the help of a little winter cloud to keep him cool. Best of all, the sisters were back together and happy at last!

MELTING
HEARTS

It was a beautiful spring day. The sun was shining over Arendelle as Anna bounced around the kitchen. She had planned a picnic for all her best friends and couldn't wait to get started.

"Are you ready?" Elsa asked, peeking into the kitchen.

"Almost," Anna said as she closed the lid of the picnic basket. "Most of the bags are in the hall, but can you grab that brown one?"

"What's in here?" Elsa asked.

"Just a few picnic essentials," Anna replied.

"You sure you have everything?" Kristoff teased. "Maybe you want to bring, perhaps ... the castle?"

Elsa and Kristoff chuckled.

"I just want everything to be perfect," Anna said.

"It'll be great," Elsa said, "because we'll all be together."

"I'm already having fun," said Kristoff.
Anna smiled as she struggled with the bags.
Kristoff quickly took them fron Anna. "Sven and I can help with those."

"Hi, everybody!" Olaf shouted as he ran towards his friends.
"Oooh. Is that a real picnic basket? I love picnics. I'm so excited!
Let's go, let's go!"

"Let the picnic begin," Anna said, leading the way to the mountains.

Anna took a deep breath. "Those spring flowers make the air smell so sweet."
"They really do," said Elsa.
"Mmmmm!" Olaf said as he sniffed a patch of flowers.

"Hey, look!" Olaf plucked a petal from one of the flowers. "It looks like a heart."
"Wow, it really does," Anna said. She smiled as they continued to walk.

Just then, something caught Anna's eye. She scooped
up a leaf and showed it off. "Hey, I found a heart, too!"
"Nice," said Elsa. Then she began searching, too.

"Found one!" Elsa called. She held up a smooth, heart-shaped stone.

"I bet I can find one," Kristoff said.

"Not before I find another." Anna grinned and raced ahead, looking for more.

Kristoff found a curved twig and bent it into the shape of a heart.
"Got one!" he said happily. But then the twig snapped in half.
Even Sven decided to join the game, too!

As the friends walked on, they continued to search for hearts.
Some things looked like broken hearts.
Others looked like perfect hearts.

And a few things ... didn't look much like hearts at all.
But all of them were fun to find!

73

When they finally arrived at their picnic spot, Kristoff and Anna worked together to surprise everyone with a huge heart.

"Glad I packed those shears," Anna said with a smile.

"Wouldn't be a picnic without 'em," Kristoff joked.

Setting the shears aside, Anna took out the blanket.
"This is the best picnic ever!" Olaf shouted as he helped to spread it out.
Anna began to unpack the bags. But she had packed so much that it took a while....

"Oh, no!" Anna cried as she looked inside the last picnic basket. She had forgotten to pack the food!

Elsa couldn't believe it. "You packed candlesticks ... but no food?"

Anna slowly nodded her head.

Just then, everyone burst out laughing – including Anna!

77

"Oh, wait – I did remember dessert!"
Anna pulled out a small box and opened it.

"Uh-oh." Anna's smile faded. Her dessert was a
melted mess! "They used to be special chocolates ...
until the sun warmed them up."

Drip. Drop. Drip. Drop. It started to rain.

"Oh, come on!" Anna shouted at the sky.

"What a wonderfully refreshing picnic shower!" Olaf said brightly.

The rain came down harder. "Quick! Under the blanket!" Anna said.

They all huddled together, trying to stay dry.

"Olaf, it's not supposed to rain on picnics," Anna said.

"But maybe it should," Olaf smiled. "The rain is keeping us close. It's like a big, cuddly group hug!"

Drip. Drip. Drip. The rain started to leak through the blanket. Anna groaned. This was not the perfect picnic she had pictured. "I'm sorry, everybody," she said. "Should we just go home?"

"The picnic's not over," Elsa said, waving her hands until an ice canopy appeared.

"Beautiful!" Olaf said.

"And practical," Kristoff added.

"Thanks, Elsa." Anna hugged her sister. "Maybe we can eat the melted chocolate ... I'm sure I brought spoons."

Elsa thought for a moment, then magically created an ice mould. "Put the chocolate into this...."

It worked! They now had heart-shaped frozen chocolate treats!

The friends sat together laughing and watching the rain
while enjoying their delicious frozen chocolate hearts.
Everyone agreed with Olaf ... it was the best picnic ever!

ACROSS THE SEA

"There's our ship, Elsa!" Anna exclaimed, peering out of the window. "Are you almost ready?"

"Just about," Elsa replied as she packed the last of her things. She smiled at her sister's eagerness, but, really, she couldn't wait to go either!

Elsa had been planning a Royal Tour to visit nearby kingdoms, and now it was time to leave! Her heart fluttered with nervous excitement.

As soon as the sisters climbed aboard their ship, the captain scurried over. "Your Majesty," he said to Elsa, "I have the itinerary you sent. But I don't think we'll make it to the first stop on time. Not with waters this still."

"Don't worry," Anna said, taking the wheel.

"We've got it covered," Elsa said, smiling. "I'll give us a little nudge." She raised her arms and created a light snow flurry, pushing the ship along at a steady pace.

"Woo-hoo!" Anna cried, the flurry blowing through her hair. "Away we go!"

Soon the ship arrived at its first port ... the kingdom of Zaria. The Zarians clapped and cheered at the sight of their visitors.

"Welcome, Queen Elsa and Princess Anna!" King Stebor called in a booming voice.

"We cannot wait to show you our kingdom," Queen Renalia added warmly.

"Thank you!" Anna and Elsa said together, bowing to their hosts.

First, the king and queen of Zaria invited the sisters to have lunch. Anna and Elsa enjoyed lively conversation and tasty food they had never tried before.

"Renalia thought I couldn't talk when we first met. I was so nervous around her," King Stebor told them.

"Oh, that's sweet!" Anna said.

"Yes, except now he won't stop talking," Queen Renalia joked playfully.

Then Anna and Elsa were taken on a tour of Zaria's prized gardens, where there were many colourful and sweet-smelling blossoms and shrubs on display.

Elsa pointed out a flower that looked remarkably like their friend, Olaf.

"We'll be sure to give you some of those seeds to take home, then," King Stebor said.

That night, they were treated to a grand festival.

"We've heard so much about your special talents," Queen Renalia said to Elsa. "Won't you show us some of your magic?"

Suddenly, Elsa felt very shy. She gave a little icy flourish with her hands and then looked at the floor.

"Would you like to join the dancing, Your Majesties?" she asked, changing the subject. "That looks like fun."

The king and queen agreed and the rest of the evening was filled with music and fun.

The next stop on Anna and Elsa's tour was a kingdom called Chatho. The sisters met Chatho's ruler, Queen Colisa, in front of her impressive palace.

"Thank you for having us, Your Majesty," Elsa said.

"Of course," the queen replied. "I am very happy you are both here!"

Queen Colisa first took the sisters on a walk through the kingdom's rainforest, where they saw many unique animals. Anna was particularly fond of some bashful furry creatures. "Why, hello there!" she cooed.

Next, the queen led Anna and Elsa into an enormous gallery.
Chatho was known for its striking art and relics.

"These are beautiful," Elsa said.

"I'm so glad you think so," Queen Colisa replied. "Would you
like to add an ice sculpture to our collection?"

Suddenly, Elsa noticed a block
of ice under a spotlight, ready to
be carved. Once again, she felt a wave
of shyness.

Noticing her sister's discomfort, Anna jumped in.
"Um ... sure! Ice sculptures are actually my speciality!"

Later, Anna gently asked Elsa why she hadn't wanted to show her powers.

"I guess I just got nervous," Elsa admitted.

Anna smiled. "Well, that's silly. You can do wonderful things." She grabbed some snow that Elsa had created earlier and placed it on her upper lip. "You can even give me a new look!"

Elsa laughed and hugged her sister. "Thanks, Anna. You're ..."

"... the Duke of Weselton!"

The sisters had arrived at their next port, only to see a familiar face. This duke had been very unkind to Elsa when her icy powers had first been revealed.

"What are you doing here?" Anna asked him. The sisters had avoided Weselton on their tour. This stop was the kingdom of Mandonia, far from Weselton.

The duke smoothed his coat as Anna and Elsa got off the ship.

"I am visiting my mother's cousin's wife's nephew, if you must know. Although I wish I hadn't. If I were you, I would turn your ship round right now."

The sisters looked at one another.

The duke sighed as he explained, "Mandonia has had the hottest summer in years. It is just unbearable! Of course, you wouldn't care about that."

"Take us to the kingdom," Elsa said firmly to the duke. Anna grinned.

As the duke led the sisters into the village, they felt as though they were stepping into a hot, sticky cloud. The Mandonians were sprawled out, sweaty and tired.

Now Elsa didn't feel shy at all. She knew she had to help these people to cool down. After she had conjured some snow clouds, Elsa saw the townspeople start to come to life.

"It's working," the duke cried in surprise.

"Why don't you get us some lemonade?" Elsa prompted him.
She started making some frosted mugs out of ice.

"Thank you, Queen Elsa. Thank you!" the crowd cheered.

Soon, Mandonia became a
frozen wonderland. The citizens even
had enough energy to slide down the new snowy piles on
wooden boards!

"I suppose a thank you is in order," the duke said begrudgingly.
"I frankly don't know where to begin...."

"Well, you could grab a board," Elsa suggested, winking at Anna.

The duke turned red. "Well ... a duke would never ... it isn't...."

"It's okay. We'll show you how it's done," Anna called, racing her
sister down the hill.

A few hours later, it was time for Anna and Elsa to return to Arendelle.
They boarded their ship and waved goodbye to their new friends.

"Did you have a good trip?" Anna asked her sister.

"I did," Elsa replied as she created a blast of snow to direct them homewards.

"I'd say that was the best Royal Tour ever ... until next time, that is!"

Olaf's Perfect Summer Day

Summer had finally arrived in Arendelle. Everyone in the kingdom was enjoying the long sunny days after a very cold winter season.

But today was going to be the hottest day of the year so far! Most of the villagers wanted to stay inside where it was cool ...

... but Olaf could hardly wait to get outside! This was the kind of day he had always wanted to experience!

Olaf ran into Princess Anna's room, calling out with excitement.
"Anna, Anna! Guess what today is? It's the perfect summer's day!
Let's go outside and play!"

Anna groaned as she sat up in bed. "It's so hot and sticky, Olaf."
But she had to smile when she saw Olaf's hopeful face.

Together, Olaf and Anna went to look for Queen Elsa. They found her in the Great Hall.

"There you are, Elsa!" Olaf cried out, joyfully. He looked up shyly at the visitor standing with Elsa. "Hi, my name is Olaf and I like warm hugs."

"H-h-hello," the visitor stuttered in surprise. He had never seen a talking snowman before!

Olaf turned back to Elsa. "And today is the best day for warm hugs because it's sunny and hot. Please can we go and play in the sunshine?"

"But it's so hot outside," Anna said. "Couldn't you cool things down just a bit, Elsa?"

"But Olaf's always wanted to experience heat," Elsa reasoned. "Let's do everything he's always wanted to do in summer!"

"How about a picnic on the shores of the fjord?" Anna suggested.

Olaf clasped his hands with glee. "Oooh, I love picnics!"

Anna, Elsa and Olaf trooped to the royal kitchens for picnic supplies.
They found Gerda with her head in the icebox.
"Gerda, what on Earth are you doing?" asked Elsa.

Gerda popped her head up. "I'm trying to keep myself cool!"
Olaf giggled. "Did you bake cookies today?"
Gerda shook her head. "Oh, it's too hot for baking."
Elsa glanced at Olaf. She didn't want him to be disappointed.
"How about an ice-cold lemonade instead?" she suggested.
Olaf was thrilled. "Oooh, I love lemonade!"

Olaf, Anna and Elsa set off outside. In the royal gardens, a few children were lying on the grass. Olaf didn't realize they were too hot to play games. He ran over to them, giggling happily.

"Hi, my name is Olaf. Don't you just love summer?" The children liked Olaf, so they joined him in chasing butterflies and blowing the fuzz off dandelions.

Even Elsa and Anna couldn't resist joining in!

After a while, Anna plopped down on the grass. "Whew! I'm ready for our picnic!" she said.

Elsa agreed. "Yes, let's head to the docks. We can sail to the fjord."

Olaf, who had been chasing a bumblebee, stopped in his tracks. "We're going sailing? I've always wanted to try sailing!"

At the docks, Anna and Elsa chose a beautiful sailing boat. As they set sail, Olaf hummed happily. He even got to steer the boat!

When they reached the shore, Olaf couldn't sit still!

"Don't you just love the feeling of sand on your snow?" he squealed. "Let's make sand angels!"

Anna gingerly stuck a toe in the hot sand. "Oh, goodness, that is ... warm!" she squeaked.

Anna danced on tiptoe over the hot sand to the fjord's edge.

"Ah, this is better," she said, as the cool water washed over her feet.

The three friends spent the
whole afternoon playing in
the summer sun.

They built sandcastles and sand people.

They chased waves on the shore.

They even danced with seagulls!

And finally, when they'd tired themselves out, Anna,
Elsa and Olaf had a picnic on the shores of the fjord.
"Hands down, this is the best day of my life," said Olaf.

As they sailed back to Arendelle, the setting sun made beautiful colours in the sky. Olaf was amazed. "I wish I could hug the summer sun. I bet it would feel wonderful!"

Anna smiled as she swept her sweaty hair off her face. "You might need a bigger snow flurry for that, Olaf!"

Back at the docks, Kristoff and Sven were waiting. They had spent the afternoon harvesting mountain lakes. Now their sledge was full of ice.

Jumping out of the boat, Anna flung herself onto the cold blocks. "Oh, am I glad to see you!"

Olaf told Kristoff and Sven all about their adventures and then sighed with happiness. "I wish it could always be summer!" he said.

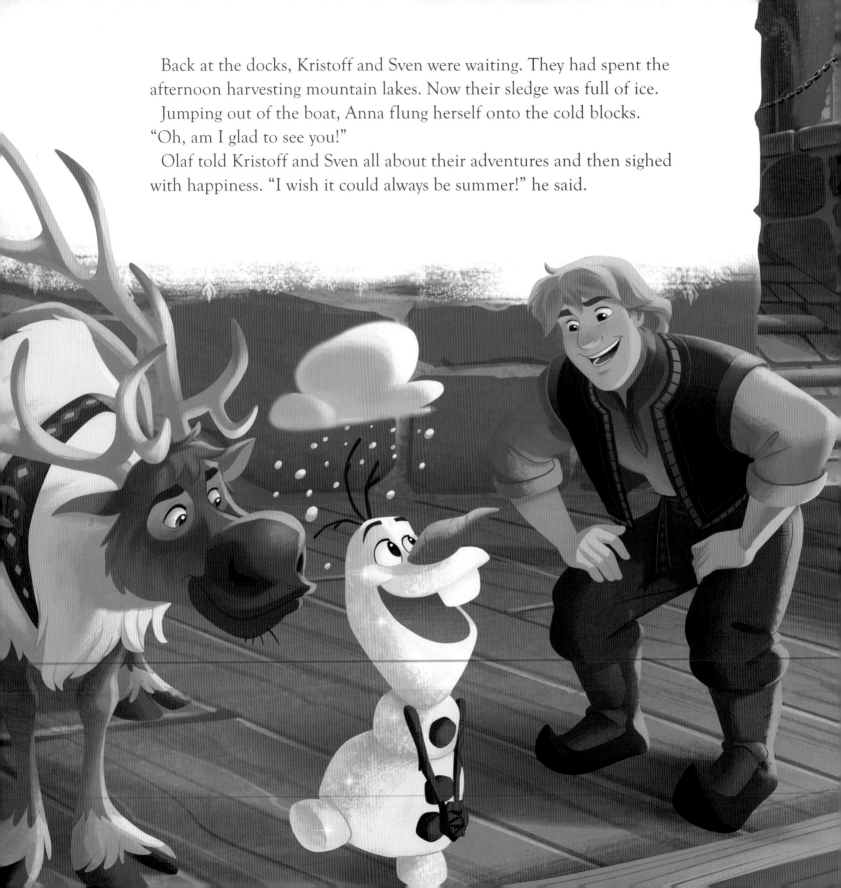

"Summer is wonderful," Elsa said with a wink.
"But I predict a chance of snow tomorrow."

Babysitting the Troll Tots

Anna pulled on her boots. Kristoff and Sven would be there any minute. They were going to visit Troll Valley to watch over the toddler trolls that evening, while the adult trolls went to their annual magical convention.

"Are you sure you don't need me to come?" Elsa asked. "I can give some magical help."

"I think we've got it covered," Anna said, giving her sister a quick hug. "They're just babies.... How hard can it be?"

Soon, Anna, Kristoff and Sven were heading off towards the setting sun. They admired the beautiful view as Kristoff told Anna stories about growing up with the sweet and silly trolls.

"I wonder if I should have brought games," Anna said. "Do trolls like games?"

"Oh, don't worry," Kristoff responded. "They'll probably sleep the whole time. I bet we'll just be relaxing by the fire, eating some snacks."

He explained that Bulda, his adoptive mother, had a very strict bedtime for all the young trolls. Sven grunted in agreement.

As soon as they reached Troll Valley, Anna and Kristoff saw dozens of mossy rocks rolling towards them. Suddenly, the trolls appeared and warmly greeted the visitors.

"Kristoff, Sven, Anna! Welcome! We missed you!" the trolls cried. Then Bulda thanked them for offering to babysit.

"It seems like just yesterday you were young enough to have a babysitter yourself, Kristoff," said Bulda. "Remember when all you wanted to do was run naked through the valley?"

"Oh, really?" Anna asked, stifling a giggle. "You never mentioned that."

"Okay, that's enough stories for now," Kristoff groaned.

Next, Bulda took Anna and Kristoff to the troll tots. "If they get hungry, you can feed them smashed berries. And they may need a leaf change. But it's just about their bedtime, so they should be sleeping soon."

Anna waved as the adult trolls left. "Have fun! Everything is going to be ..."

"... a disaster!"

Anna, Kristoff and Sven turned to see the toddler trolls escaping from their pen. They were running, climbing and swinging all over the place.

"Oh ... no, no!" Anna said, rushing to the trolls who were climbing on top of massive boulders. "That's dangerous."

Kristoff ran to a leaning tower of trolls that had just sprouted.

"All right, guys," Kristoff said, gently pulling the trolls off one another. "Let's settle down now."

But the more Kristoff, Anna and Sven tried to calm the little trolls, the wilder they became!

"Maybe they're hungry," Anna said, heading for the basket of smashed berries. "Yummy!" she cooed, while Sven tried to show them just how tasty the food was. But the little trolls seemed to have better things to do.

"Maybe they need changing?" Kristoff suggested. He bravely peered into one of the troll's nappy leaves. "Nope."

"Let's put them to bed," Anna suggested. "They must be tired by now."

But, alas, the young trolls were wide awake.

Suddenly, a cheery voice interrupted them.
"Hello, troll babies!"
It was their friend, Olaf!

"Elsa sent me in case you needed some help," Olaf explained to Anna and Kristoff, before turning to the excited trolls. "Why, hi there! Ha, ha! That tickles!"

"Boy, are we glad to see you," Kristoff said.

Anna ran to greet the snowman. But in her hurry, she tripped, falling face-first into the basket of berries! "Whoaaa!"

Kristoff rushed over to her side. "Anna! Are you okay?"

Anna lifted her head,
her face covered in
dripping purple goo.

The little trolls burst into loud giggles.
They stampeded towards her, lapping
up the berry juice from her cheeks!
Anna laughed. "Well, I guess this is
one way to feed them."

151

After the trolls were done, they sat in a heap, happy and full. Suddenly, a strange smell floated into the air. The trolls looked down at their leaves.

"Uh-oh," Kristoff said knowingly. "Olaf, you distract them."

Olaf happily told the little trolls stories about his most favourite thing in the world – summer. Anna and Sven collected leaves, while Kristoff changed nappies. Soon everyone was clean and sweet-smelling once more.

"And now for a song about summer!" Olaf announced.

Anna noticed that the trolls were swaying. Some of them were having trouble keeping their eyes open.

"Actually," she said, "maybe Kristoff and Sven would like to sing a lullaby instead."

"Good thing I brought my lute," Kristoff replied, while Anna and Olaf put the trolls to bed.

"Rock-a-bye troll-ys, in your small pen," Kristoff sang.

"Time to go sleepy for Uncle Sven," Kristoff continued, this time pretending to be Sven.

By the time the adult trolls returned, the wee ones were sound asleep.

"Wow, great job," Bulda whispered.

"It was easy," Anna replied, nudging Kristoff.

"Piece of mud pie," Kristoff added.

"You two will be great parents some day!" said Bulda.

Anna and Kristoff looked at each other and smiled.

THE END